Koen Van Biesen has illustrated over twenty children's books. He lives in Belgium and teaches at the Academy of Fine Arts in Mortsel. Visit his website at www.koenvanbiesen.com.

For Muriel

First published in the United States in 2015 by
Eerdmans Books for Young Readers
an imprint of Wm. B. Eerdmans Publishing Co.
2140 Oak Industrial Dr. NE
Grand Rapids, Michigan 49505
P.O. Box 163, Cambridge CB3 9PU U.K.

www.eerdmans.com/youngreaders

Originally published in Belgium in 2013 under the title
Buurman Leest Een Boek
by Uitgeverij De Eenhoorn bvba, Vlasstraat 17,
B-8710 Wielsbeke, Belgium

Text and illustrations © 2012 Koen Van Biesen
© 2012 Uitgeverij De Eenhoorn bvba
English language translation © 2015 Laura Watkinson

Manufactured at Tien Wah Press in Malaysia

22 21 20 19 18 17 16 15   9 8 7 6 5 4 3 2 1

Library of Congress Cataloging-in-Publication Data

Van Biesen, Koen, 1964- author, illustrator.
[Buurman leest een boek. English]
Roger is reading a book / Koen Van Biesen;
[translated by Laura Watkinson].
pages cm
Summary: "Roger wants some peace and quiet so he can read his book,
but his neighbor Emily has some hobbies of her own — very loud ones!"
Provided by publisher.
ISBN 978-0-8028-5442-1
[1. Books and reading — Fiction. 2. Noise — Fiction.]
I. Watkinson, Laura, translator. II. Title.
PZ7.1.V36Rog 2015
[E] — dc23
2014031302

Flemish Literature Fund

The translation of this book was funded by the Flemish Literature Fund.

The illustrations were created using mixed media.
The display and text type was set in Bureau Grotesque.

FSC
www.fsc.org

MIX
Paper from responsible sources
FSC® C012700

ROGER

IS READING
A BOOK

Koen Van Biesen

Translated by
Laura Watkinson

Eerdmans Books for Young Readers

Grand Rapids, Michigan • Cambridge, U.K.

SHHHH!

Quiet.
**Roger is reading.
Roger is reading a book.**

BOING BOING

Emily is playing.
Emily is playing a game.

KNOCK

Roger knocks.

SHHHH!

Quiet.
Roger is reading.
Roger is reading a book.

LA LA LA

Emily is singing.
Emily is singing a song.

KNOCKITY KNOCK

Roger knocks.
Noisily.

SHHHH!

Quiet.
Roger is reading.
Roger is reading a book.

BOOM

Emily is playing.
Emily is playing the drum.

BOOM BOOM
BOOM

KNOCK
KNOCK
KNOCKITY KNOCK

Roger knocks. Really noisily.

POK
POK
POK

TRIP

TRIP TRIP

TRAP

BAF

BAF

BAF

BAF

SHHHh!

Is Roger reading?
No, Roger is not reading now.

Book down.
Coat on.
Scarf on.
Light off.

Roger has made up his mind.

KNOCK KNOCK KNOCK

Package.
A package from Roger.

OH...

A book.

SHHHH! Quiet.

Emily is reading. Emily is reading a book.

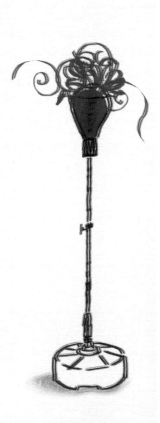

SHHHH! Quiet.

Roger is reading. Roger is reading a book.

Quiet.

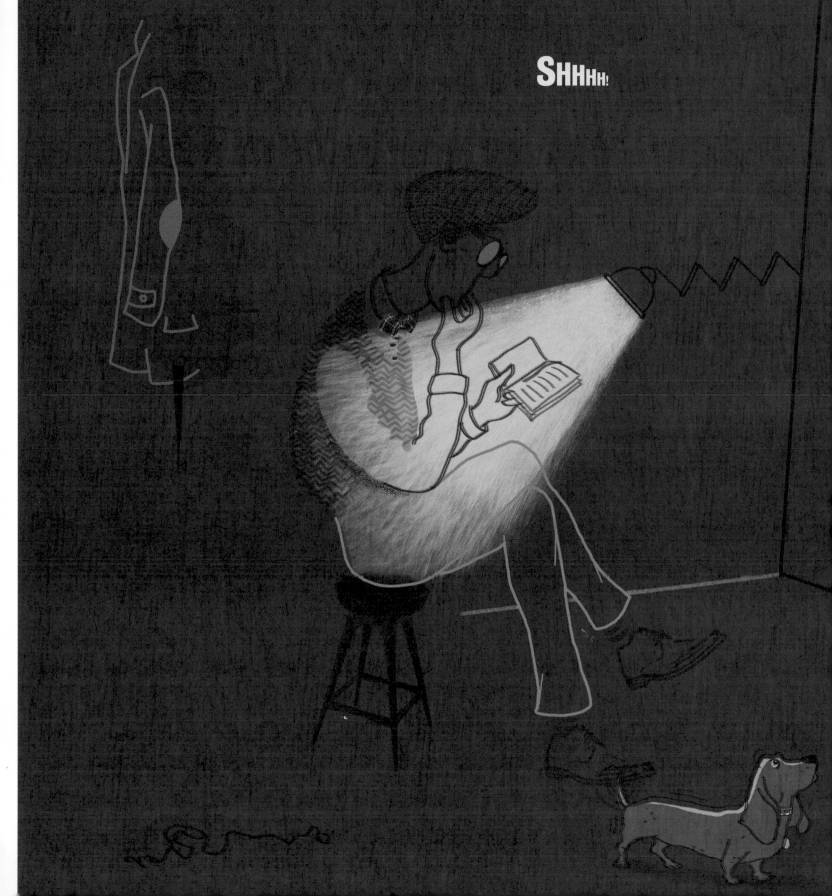